BALLPARK®
Mysteries 14

THE
CARDINALS
CAPER

Also by David A. Kelly
BALLPARK MYSTERIES®

THE MVP SERIES

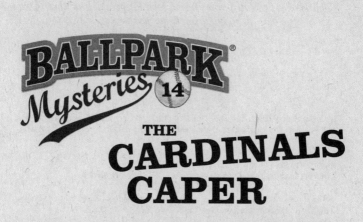

Ballpark Mysteries 14

THE CARDINALS CAPER

by David A. Kelly

illustrated by Mark Meyers

A STEPPING STONE BOOK™
Random House 🏠 New York

This book is dedicated to my friend John Fitzgerald, who's been a huge St. Louis Cardinals fan forever.
—D.A.K.

"It ain't bragging if you can do it."
—Dizzy Dean, St. Louis Cardinals pitcher, 1930, 1932–1937

Text copyright © 2018 by David A. Kelly
Cover art and interior illustrations copyright © 2018 by Mark Meyers

Visit us on the Web!
SteppingStonesBooks.com
rhcbooks.com

Educators and librarians, for a variety of teaching tools,
visit us at RHTeachersLibrarians.com

Library of Congress Cataloging-in-Publication Data
Kelly, David A.
The Cardinals caper / by David A. Kelly ; illustrated by Mark Meyers.
p. cm.—(Ballpark mysteries ; 14)
"A Stepping Stone Book."
Summary: When a beloved Dalmatian goes missing while cousins Mike and Kate are in St. Louis for a Cardinals game, they rush to investigate and find a ransom note.
ISBN 978-1-5247-6751-8 (trade)—ISBN 978-1-5247-6752-5 (lib. bdg.)—
ISBN 978-1-5247-6753-2 (ebook)
[1. St. Louis Cardinals (Baseball team)—Fiction. 2. Baseball—Fiction. 3. Cousins—Fiction. 4. Extortion—Fiction. 5. Mystery and detective stories. 6. Saint Louis (Mo.)—Fiction.] I. Meyers, Mark, illustrator. II. Title.
PZ7.K2936 Car 2018 [Fic]—dc23 2017007673

Printed in the United States of America
10 9 8 7 6 5 4 3 2 1

This book has been officially leveled by using the F&P Text Level Gradient™ Leveling System.

Contents

A Great Escape

Kate Hopkins reached up and gently petted the nose of a big brown horse. It nuzzled her hand.

Kate giggled. The horse lifted its head and whinnied. It had a white stripe on its nose and white feet.

"Don't get your arm bitten off, or we'll miss the game!" her cousin Mike Walsh said. He was tossing a baseball from one hand to the other. "Red Gibson is going to set the Cardinals' hitting streak record tonight! He's hit in thirty-three straight games so far."

Kate reached back up to pet the horse again. "It's okay, Mike. We're not going to miss any of the action," she said.

The horse and five other Clydesdale horses were hitched to a tall red delivery wagon with big white wheels. At the beginning of the baseball game, the horses would pull the wagon inside the stadium while a bouncy "oompah-pah" song played. The Clydesdales appeared at

St. Louis Cardinals games on special occasions and for the first and last games of the season. They were at today's game for the Cardinals' Lewis and Clark Days celebration.

"Don't worry," the horse team driver said to Mike. "Duke doesn't bite." The driver wore bright green pants with yellow stripes down the side and a crisp white shirt with a black tie. A name tag on his shirt read MANNY. Manny

reached over and gave Duke a pat. "Well, maybe he'd bite you if you were a Pittsburgh Pirates fan!" he joked.

Manny's partner, Tommy, laughed. Tommy was polishing the wagon. He was dressed like Manny. "We don't have to worry about the Pirates tonight," Tommy said. "Red Gibson is sure to continue his hitting streak."

It was six o'clock in the evening. Mike and Kate were in the groundskeepers' area in the Cardinals' stadium. Kate's mother, Mrs. Hopkins, had arranged for the kids to visit with the horses. She was a sports reporter and often brought Mike and Kate with her to games.

People bustled all around them. Grounds-keepers were fetching rakes and supplies. On the other side of a garage door was the stadium's outfield. A groundskeeper with a mustache stood just inside the door, dipping pretzels into a jar of peanut butter and munching on them as he watched the other groundskeepers. He seemed to be the boss.

The noise of the fans finding their seats flooded in through the open doorway. Nearby, Manny and Tommy were getting the horses ready for their appearance on the field.

"Let's get a photo!" Kate said.

Mike pulled out his phone. But before he could take the picture, he noticed a baseball player on the other side of the wagon.

"Hey, it's Red Gibson!" Mike said. "What are you doing here?"

Red stood tall in his St. Louis uniform. He had a bushy black beard and long arms and legs. His young face looked friendly. He smiled at Mike and Kate and walked over to shake their hands.

"Hello there!" he said. "I came down for a

good-luck visit before the game. I do a lot of charity events with Manny and Tommy, and I like to spend time with the animals."

Manny laughed. "You don't just like these animals; you *love* them!" he said. He looked at Mike and Kate. "I've never met someone who loves animals more. He's even studying to be a veterinarian when he retires from baseball." Manny patted the side of the old-fashioned delivery wagon. "I know someone who's going to be thrilled to see you, Red."

WHEEET! WOOO!

Manny gave a loud whistle. A black-and-white blur flashed down from the driver's seat of the wagon. Mike and Kate felt something brush past their legs.

Two big paws landed on Red's chest, and a long pink tongue darted out to lick the side of his face!

"Louie!" Red called out. "That's my boy! You're my special good-luck charm!"

Louie, a large Dalmatian, continued to lick and nuzzle Red. Red petted the dog's back. "As long as you're here, I know I'll be able to set a new hitting record!" he said. "Maybe I should see if Coach can make you the mascot for our team!"

Manny held up his hand. "Not so fast, Red," he said. "We need Louie to travel with the horses. Dalmatians have always helped keep the horses calm."

Tommy stood up from cleaning the wheels of the wagon. "That's not a bad idea," he said. "If Red keeps Louie, we can focus on the horses. Maybe we can get a stuffed Dalmatian."

Manny shook his head. "That's a horrible idea, Tommy!" he said. "The horses love Louie. Red's not getting the dog."

Tommy shrugged and went back to work. "Whatever," he mumbled.

Red gave Louie one more hug. "Down, boy," he said. Louie dropped to the ground and looked at Mike and Kate.

"I think Louie would like to meet you," Red said. "Shake!"

Louie sat and then held up his paw for Mike to shake.

Mike laughed. "Oh, you're trying to teach me a trick, are you?" he said. Mike shook Louie's paw. "Nice to meet you!"

"Attaboy!" Red said. He let Louie give him another lick and a handshake. "I'd love to stay here with you, but I have a game to play. And since you're my favorite furry friend, I'm going to set a hitting record for you tonight!"

Mike held out his baseball and pulled a marker from his back pocket. "Red! Would you be willing to sign my ball first?" he asked.

Red smiled. "Sure!" he said. He took Mike's ball and signed his name across its sweet spot. Then he handed it back to Mike.

"Thanks!" Mike said.

"No problem," Red said. He waved goodbye and disappeared into a hallway.

"That was so cool to meet Red Gibson!" Kate said. "And Louie!" She gave the dog a hug and then checked the time. "We need to get going," she said. "Let's find our seats so we can watch Louie, Duke, and the rest of the horses parade around the field before the game!"

As Mike and Kate turned to leave, one of the Cardinals clubhouse attendants walked by and opened a door to the loading zone outside.

Louie pricked up his ears. The last rays of sunlight shone through the open door. At the sight, Louie took off in a flash.

"Hey, look out!" Kate called.

Before anyone could grab him, Louie dashed out the door!

Dog Gone!

Louie's tail disappeared around the corner.

"Quick, get him!" Manny called. He dropped the rag he was using to polish the wagon and ran after the dog. Mike and Kate looked at Tommy, but he just shook his head, shrugged, and went back to polishing the wagon.

"Come on," Kate said. "We've got to catch Louie!" She and Mike started to run after Manny. Then a wet black nose poked in around the edge of the door.

It was Louie!

The dog ran over to Kate, sat down, and looked up at her.

"Aww," Kate said. She knelt and gave him a hug. "That's a good dog," she said. "You don't want to escape! You'll miss the game and Red setting his big record!"

Manny walked through the door. A man in a white chef's hat followed behind him. "Louie was too fast for me, but luckily Harry here stopped him before he ran through the gate into the street," Manny said. He pointed to a red-and-white-striped hot dog cart near the door to the hallway. A sign across the top read GOOD DOGS! "Harry is our hot dog king! He comes down here before games to feed the grounds crew."

Harry waved at Mike and Kate. In his other hand, he was carrying a phone. "Happy to help," he said. "I was outside making a phone call when Louie zoomed past me. But I was able to catch up and stop him. I guess it takes a hot dog guy to catch a *hot* dog! Get it?"

Manny laughed. "That's good, Harry," he said. "Save a hot dog for me! I'll take one after we put the horses on the trucks."

"I will, but you'll have to get it before the second inning. That's when I move up near the main entrance," Harry said. He sniffled a few times, then turned his head and sneezed.

Manny glanced over at Tommy, who was checking the horses' harnesses. "Hey, Tommy," he said. "Thanks for the help! I just love the way you jumped up to catch Louie. Oh, wait—you didn't!"

Tommy looked at Manny and shrugged. "I knew you'd catch him," he said. "Louie never goes very far. Besides, I've told you a thousand times, I think we should leave Louie at the stables. We have our hands full taking care of the horses."

Manny looked at Mike and Kate and sighed. "Tommy's a great partner, but he's not really a dog person," he said. "He's more of a horse person."

"I like Louie!" Tommy said. "I just don't think we need him on the road with us."

Mike dropped to his knees near Kate. He put his ball on the ground and petted Louie. "And I like you, too, Louie!" Mike said.

Harry stepped over to look at the ball. "Is that a signed ball?" he asked. Before Mike could answer, Harry let out a loud sneeze. He pointed at Louie. "Sorry," he said. "I'm a little bit allergic to dogs." He picked up Mike's baseball. "Red Gibson? You have a signed Red Gibson ball?"

Mike nodded. "Yup. He was here a little while ago and signed it for me."

Harry let out a low whistle. "That's great!" he said. "I'd love to have one of these for my Cardinals collection. I'm a huge fan." Harry studied the baseball. "It will be even more valuable after tonight!"

Harry flipped the ball back to Mike. "Enjoy the game!" he said. "I've got to get back to selling the dogs. Catch you later! Get it? *Catch you later?* Like the dog I just caught?" Harry laughed and then headed back to his cart, sneezing on the way. Two of the groundskeepers were waiting for hot dogs.

Kate stood up. "We need to get to our seats before the game starts!" she said to Tommy and Manny. "Thanks for letting us pet the horses and visit with Louie!"

Mike and Kate waved goodbye and walked through the stadium. Kate's mother had bought them tickets in the first row, right along the third-base line.

"There's the Arch!" Mike said as they plopped down in their seats. He pointed past the center-field seats to the huge silver Gateway Arch, which was about six blocks away. The 630-foot-high structure towered over the ballpark. Mike and Kate could just make out the small windows of the visitors' area at the top.

"It was really cool going up there this morning," Kate said. She and Mike had taken a small five-person tram car up to the top, where they looked out at the city. Mike hadn't liked how cramped the tram car was, but he loved the view of the city and the fact that he could look right into the Cardinals' stadium.

Mike pointed to the visitors' area. "I still think we should have watched the game from up there," he said. "Then we wouldn't have had to buy tickets!"

Before Kate could respond, the loudspeakers blared with organ music. A door in the right-field wall rolled open, and out marched the horses!

Duke led the hitch of Clydesdales pulling the delivery wagon. Manny and Tommy sat on the open seat in the front. And right between them was Louie! Even from far away, Mike and Kate could see Louie's tail wag as they rolled along the inside wall of the stadium.

The crowd cheered wildly. Mike and Kate stood up with the fans and clapped along in time to the music. The horses rounded the out-field warning track and headed for home plate.

As the wagon passed the seats near the visitors' dugout on the third-base side, Mike and Kate jumped up and down and called out, "Louie! Louie! Louie!"

Manny and Tommy waved back at the crowd while steering the horses. Just as the wagon went past Mike and Kate, they heard an excited noise.

WOOF! WOOF! WOOF!

Louie was barking at them from the top of the wagon! He had spotted them in the crowd.

When the parade ended and the wagon left the field a few minutes later, Mike turned to Kate and gave her a high five.

"That was cool!" Kate said. "Louie really looked like he was having a good time."

"I know!" Mike said. "Once Red starts hitting, we'll *all* have a good time."

After the national anthem, the Cardinals took the field to huge cheers. When the crowd quieted, Mike and Kate sat down for the start of the game.

The first Pirates batter stepped up to the plate and took a few practice swings. The Cardinals pitcher glared at him and nodded to the catcher. A moment later, he hurled a fastball at the plate.

WHACK!

The ball zoomed high into the air. The Pirates player dropped the bat and ran for first.

The ball climbed higher. The runner rounded first and headed for second. The ball flew farther and farther. The fans in the stadium grew quiet.

"Oh no!" Kate said.

The ball sailed over the outfield fence. It was a home run!

The runner rounded third and cruised home. He crossed the plate and gave his teammates fist bumps when he returned to the dugout. With just one pitch the Cardinals were behind, 1–0!

As the next batter came to the plate, the Cardinals fans cheered. They weren't going to let one run stop them.

The cheers seemed to work. The Cardinals pitcher struck out the second and third batters, and the fourth one grounded out. The inning was half over! No more runs were scored.

As the Cardinals players ran off the field to get ready to bat, Kate's phone rang. She answered it and talked for a minute. When she hung up, she turned to Mike. "That was my mom," she said. "Manny asked her to call us."

"Why?" Mike asked. "What's going on?"

Kate stood up and tugged on Mike's shirt. "We have to go," she said. "Louie is missing!"

A Note

"Louie escaped again?" Mike asked.

"Yes!" Kate said. "My mom said that Manny called her looking for us. Louie disappeared, and Manny thought we might be able to help find him since Louie liked us so much. We've got to get back down to the groundskeepers' area right away!"

Mike glanced at the field. The Cardinals were getting ready to bat. Red would be up soon. "Okay, let's go!" he said. "But when we find Louie, let's put him on a leash!"

Mike and Kate ran through the hallways of the stadium. They took an elevator to a lower level and ran down a long hallway. The security guards waved them through a checkpoint. Soon, Mike and Kate were back in the room where they had seen the team of horses.

But Manny and Tommy weren't there!

The room was empty. There were no horses, no dog, no people. Just piles of dirt and grass seed for the field. At the far end of the room was a small workshop with tools and cabinets. A fan rattled overhead. A collection of lawn mowers and other machines lined one wall.

"Manny! Tommy!" Kate called.

"We're in the loading area!" came a voice from outside.

Mike pointed to the open door that Louie had escaped through earlier. He and Kate walked into a large loading zone lit with streetlights.

The lot was fenced off from the street. Highway traffic rumbled above them.

Manny and Tommy were standing next to a long tractor trailer with big pictures of the horses on its side.

"Mike! Kate!" Manny called out. "Over here!"

The cousins ran over. "What happened?" Kate asked.

Manny sighed. He pointed to the area that Mike and Kate had just come from. "After we finished parading around the stadium, we unhitched the horses in there," he said. "Louie was lying on a mat next to the wagon. He always does that. He likes to rest after his ride."

Tommy patted the side of the tractor trailer. "We opened our truck and led the horses in one by one, just like we always do," he said. He pointed to another tractor trailer standing behind the first one. "Then we loaded the delivery wagon on that truck and secured it."

"We were just about to leave when we realized we couldn't find Louie. We searched everywhere, but he was nowhere to be seen," Manny said. "He's always ready to go when the truck is ready. He likes to ride up front with us."

Mike and Kate looked around. There were lots of places for a dog to hide outside the stadium. But the loading area was fenced off, so

there didn't seem to be any way for Louie to escape into the city streets.

"Are you sure he's not in one of the trucks?" Mike asked. "Or with the horses?"

"We checked twice. He's not there. We also called for him," Manny said. "But he didn't come. That's why we need your help. I thought maybe Louie would come if you called him."

"We'll help you look," Kate said.

Mike and Kate began their search. "Louie!

Louie! Louie!" they called out. Kate checked around the tractor trailer trucks. Mike examined the fences for any holes. They continued to call out and search for Louie, but there was no sign of the dog.

"We should look inside," Mike said. "Maybe he ran up the hallway. We can ask the security guard if she's seen him."

"Good idea," Manny said.

Tommy held up his hand. "You guys can look inside," he said. Tommy glanced at Manny. "Louie is your responsibility. I need to take care of the horses."

Tommy walked over to the horse truck and went inside. Manny shook his head. "Tommy's great, but he *can* get a little bit grumpy," he said. "Come on, let's check with the security guard."

Manny, Kate, and Mike went back to the groundskeepers' area. Even though they couldn't see the field from inside, they could hear the Cardinals fans in the stadium and the loudspeaker announcements. "Now batting: Red Gibson!" called the announcer.

"Aw, we're going to miss Red's hit!" Mike said.

Kate waved her hand. "He'll be up again at least two more times," she said. "It's more important for us to find Louie."

Kate pointed to the security guard at the end of the hall. "Mike and I will double-check this room," she said. "You can talk with the security guard."

Manny nodded. "Sounds good," he said. He walked up the hallway to the guard, while Mike and Kate searched the room. They explored the area at the far end, near the lawn equipment. But Louie wasn't there, either. As Kate searched the workshop filled with tools,

Mike looked around where the wagon and Louie's mat had been.

"Hey, there's something here," he said, leaning down. Kate rushed over. There was a light brown streak on the ground. Mike knelt and sniffed it, his face almost touching the floor.

"What in the world are you doing?" Kate asked.

Mike smiled. "Check this out! It's peanut

butter. Crunchy. My favorite!" He rubbed his belly. "That reminds me, I'm hungry!"

Just then, Manny came back. "No sign of Louie," he said. "The guard has been there since before the game. She said there's no chance Louie went up the hallway."

"Maybe we should look outside again," Mike said.

"He's not out there," Kate said. "We both looked all around."

Mike shrugged. "Well, I'm going to double-check!" he said. He walked to the outside door and was just about to go through it when he spotted something on the floor against the wall.

"Hang on!" Mike said. He crouched down. "There's a piece of paper here with tape on it." Mike lifted it up from the floor and turned it over. There was a note on the other side. "Manny!" he shouted. "Come quick! Louie's in trouble!"

Dog-Napped

Mike held out the note. Kate's and Manny's eyes grew wide as they read the message:

I love Louie, but I love the Cardinals and their World Series wins more! So I'll make a trade: Leave a Cardinals' World Series trophy in a paper bag outside the stadium behind the statue of Stan Musial, with no security around, and I'll give Louie back. But if you don't

*drop the trophy off at the end of the
ninth inning, you'll never see Louie
again!*

"Oh no!" Manny said. "This is horrible.
Louie's been kidnapped!"

"I think the word is *dog-napped*," Mike said.
"Like in *101 Dalmatians*."

"That would be bad!" Kate said. "Cruella
de Vil wanted to make those Dalmatians into
coats! We can't let anyone do that to Louie!"

Mike scanned the room. "We won't," he said.
"If someone left a note, they might have left a
clue. Let's search this room again."

"Yes, good idea," Manny said. "But I've
got to tell Tommy about this. And then I'm
going to find Mr. Lee, the Cardinals chief of
security, to ask for help."

Mike tapped his sneaker on the ground. He

bit his lip and looked at Kate until Manny disappeared through the door.

"What if *Tommy* kidnapped Louie?" he asked.

"Tommy?" Kate asked. "Why would he do it?"

"Maybe he's trying to make his life easier by making Louie disappear," Mike said. "Think about it. Tommy doesn't like dogs. And he didn't seem to care when Louie escaped outside before the game."

Kate thought for a moment. Then she shook her head. "I really don't think so," she said. "He might like horses better than dogs, but it seems like a stretch that Tommy would kidnap Louie."

"Well, *I* think he's a suspect," Mike said. "Let's keep an eye on him while we look for clues."

"Okay," Kate said. She glanced up the hallway. "Since the guard didn't see Louie, we know he didn't go that way," she said. "Let's take one more pass through this room in case we missed anything."

Kate and Mike zigzagged across the room. But all they found were grass clippings and bits of red clay from the warning track. They stopped when they reached the far wall.

Kate frowned. "Whoever took Louie *must* have left some clues," she said.

"I know!" Mike said. "But where? And where's Manny? I thought he'd be back from talking to Tommy by now. Maybe they discovered something! Let's go find them."

BRIIING! BRIIING! BRIIING!

A telephone on the wall at the other end of the room rang.

"I'll get it!" Mike said. He started for the phone.

"Hang on!" Kate said. "It's probably for the groundskeepers."

Mike and Kate looked around. There were no groundskeepers in sight.

BRIIING! BRIIING! BRIIING!

"Okay, then," Kate said. "If no one else is going to answer it, I think we can."

Mike ran across the room and picked up the receiver.

"Hello," he said. "It's Mike Walsh."

His eyes grew wide. He looked at Kate and pointed to the phone. Then he twisted the receiver away from his mouth and said, "It's Red Gibson!"

When Mike hung up and walked back to Kate, he was shaking his head.

"Red heard from someone on the grounds crew that Louie was missing," Mike said. "He was worried and wanted to know if anyone had found him."

"Did you tell him about the note?" Kate asked.

Mike nodded. "I had to," he said. "He asked if we'd found any clues."

"How did he take it?" Kate asked.

"Not well," Mike said. "Red was really upset that Louie had been dog-napped. I hope it doesn't mess up his game!"

A Doggone Dead End

"Come on!" Kate said. "We can't let Louie's disappearance interfere with Red's hitting streak. We've got to find Manny and see what's going on."

The cool night air hit Mike and Kate as they walked outside. Streetlights lit the loading zone, but the sky was dark.

VROOM!

The tractor trailer loaded with horses pulled away from the parking area. A security guard waved to the driver as the truck drove off. The guard rolled the loading zone gates closed after the truck had passed by.

Mike and Kate waved their arms. "Wait! What about Louie?" they shouted over the noise of the truck. "Come back!"

The truck rumbled off into the night.

Mike's and Kate's shoulders slumped.

"I can't believe Manny and Tommy just left!" Mike said.

"I know!" Kate said. "Now what?"

"No! No! It's okay," said a voice.

It was Manny! He walked out from behind the other tractor trailer.

"Tommy had to get the horses back to the stables," Manny said. "He left me behind to search for Louie."

"We've looked everywhere," Kate said. "There's no sign of him."

"I know," Manny said. "Now that I've finished helping Tommy, I'm going to find Mr. Lee. I can't search the entire stadium, even with you two helping. Plus, the Cardinals have to be involved if we need a World Series trophy for the ransom."

Mike glanced at Kate. He pointed at the truck disappearing into the distance. Kate nodded.

"What if *Tommy* had something to do with Louie's disappearance?" Mike asked. "Tommy really doesn't seem to like him. Maybe he made Louie disappear."

Manny's mouth dropped open a little. Then he shook his head. "That's an interesting idea," he said. "But I know that Tommy loves Louie. He wouldn't have taken him for the ransom, or anything else. Plus, Tommy just left with the horses, so he won't be here in the ninth inning to pick up the ransom!"

"Oh," Mike said. "Well, it seemed like he doesn't care for Louie."

Manny waved his hand. "No, he does," he said. "You should see them back at the stables. He gives Louie treats all the time. Tommy just gets grumpy when we're out parading and he has to care for the horses *and* watch Louie."

"Well, if Tommy didn't take Louie, we need to figure out who did!" Kate said.

"I don't think we have time to figure that out now," Manny said. "It would be great to catch the criminal, but I really want to get Louie back. *That's* the most important thing, even if the Cardinals have to give up a trophy to do it."

Kate snapped her fingers. A big smile spread across her face. "But maybe we can figure out a way to do both," she said. "What if we could get Louie back *and* catch the criminal? All without giving up a World Series trophy!"

Manny tilted his head and stared at Kate. "How could we do that?" he asked.

"Well, the note said to leave the trophy in a bag by the Stan Musial statue with no security around," Kate said. "What if you do that, but have the Cardinals put security people across the street and at the corners?"

"But how would that help catch the dog-napper?" Mike asked. "Won't he or she get lost in the crowd?"

"Yes, for a little bit. But here's what we can do. When banks get robbed, tellers sometimes put an exploding dye packet in the bag with the money. Then, about ten seconds after the robber leaves the bank, the packet explodes and covers the robber with bright red dye. If we ask the police to put a dye packet in the bag with the trophy, the dog-napper will be easy to find even if security people aren't close by!"

Manny nodded. "That's a great idea, Kate," he said. "I'll see if Mr. Lee can arrange that. Then we'd be able to catch the dog-napper, save the trophy, and rescue Louie!"

"Perfect!" Mike said. He gave Kate a fist bump. "Way to go!"

"Thanks," she said. "Manny, while you're working on that, Mike and I will continue to investigate. How can we get ahold of you if we find something?"

Manny handed Kate a business card. "Here's my number," he said. "Call or text me if you come up with anything. I'll see what I can do."

Mike and Kate followed Manny inside. As they headed up the hallway back into the main part of the stadium, they ran into Harry, the hot dog king.

"Oh, hi, guys!" Harry said. *"Relish* a hot dog? If you do, I'm up near the main entrance. Stop by my stand. I was just coming down to get the charger for my phone. I left it plugged into the wall."

Mike and Kate shook their heads. "We can't think about eating now. Louie is missing!" Mike said. "Someone left a ransom note, and we're trying to find him."

"Oh no!" Harry said. "That's awful!"

"Did you see anything when you were selling

hot dogs here earlier?" Kate asked Harry.

"No," Harry said. "I brought my cart up to the main entrance in the first inning. When I left, Louie was lying on a mat near the wagon. Is there anything I can do to help? Maybe if we leave out some hot dogs, he'll find his way back."

"We just searched the area," Kate said. "Louie's definitely not here, so I don't think the hot dogs would help."

"Thanks, Harry," Manny said. "But I'm heading upstairs to try to arrange the ransom. We have to set it up before the ninth inning or, the note said, we won't see Louie again."

Harry sighed. "This is bad," he said. "I hope you'll be able to rescue Louie. I'd hate to see anything happen to him."

Manny nodded. "Me too," he said. "We can't replace Louie."

"Good luck!" Harry said. "I'll keep my eye out for anything strange."

Harry walked into the groundskeepers' area and unplugged his phone charger. Mike, Kate, and Manny continued up the hallway. Once they passed the security guard, Manny waved goodbye and headed for the stairs to the security office.

Mike and Kate stepped into the main walkway. Fans were streaming by to visit the restroom or buy food. Mike and Kate pushed through the crowds to the railing overlooking the field. It was the bottom of the sixth inning. St. Louis was still behind by one. There was a man on first and two outs. But at least Red would be up next if the current Cardinals batter didn't strike out.

"Now what?" Mike asked. "Tommy's gone.

We don't have any real clues. Maybe it's time to get something to eat."

Kate shook her head. "Not yet," she said. "There's still something we can investigate."

Mike raised an eyebrow. "What do you mean?" he asked.

"Maybe one of the groundskeepers took Louie!" Kate said.

A New Plan

Mike looked at the field. "The groundskeepers?" he asked.

Kate nodded. "They have lots of equipment in that area," she said. "Maybe they were there when the horses and wagon got back. One of them could have dog-napped Louie when Manny and Tommy were loading the horses on the truck."

"What a good idea! We need to check it out," Mike said. Then he looked up for a moment. "Hey, that might actually be a *great* idea!"

"What do you mean?" Kate asked as she twirled a strand of her long brown hair around her finger.

"When you said 'groundskeepers,' I just remembered we saw one when we first went to visit the horses," Mike said. "He was standing near the door to the field and *he was eating peanut butter*! Maybe we could see if it matched the peanut butter I found on the ground!"

"How would we do that?" Kate asked. "How can we *match* peanut butter?"

"It's easy," Mike said. "Crunchy or creamy! The stuff I found on the ground was crunchy. It had bits of peanuts in it. If we can find the jar of peanut butter that groundskeeper was eating, we can see if it matches."

Suddenly, the crowd roared. With one man on base and two outs, the Cardinals batter had hit a single!

"Hang on," Mike said. "Red's up next! We've got to watch this. He might set a new record!" Mike clapped and cheered with the rest of the crowd. "Let's go, Cardinals!" he yelled.

Kate jumped up and down. "Let's go, Cardinals!" she said. "*¡Vamos los Cardenales!*" Kate was teaching herself Spanish and liked to practice it whenever she could.

Mike smiled. *"¡Vamos los Cardenales!"* he yelled.

Mike and Kate stamped their feet and cheered with the rest of the fans as Red left the dugout to bat.

But Red took his time walking to the plate. He seemed to be scanning the crowd on his way. Finally, he spotted Mike and Kate. He

pointed at them and held up his hands for a moment.

"He pointed at us!" Kate said.

"I think he wants to know if we found Louie!" Mike said. "What do we say?"

"The only thing we *can* say—the truth," Kate said. She shook her head at Red. Then she shrugged, held up her hands, and mouthed the word *sorry*.

Red's shoulders drooped. He nodded and continued to walk to the plate. He took a couple of deep breaths and then swung his bat back and forth. Red ground his front foot into the dirt, stared out at the pitcher, and waited.

The Pirates pitcher waited for the right sign from the catcher. He shook off one after another but then got one he liked. A moment later, the ball zoomed toward the plate.

Red stood still. The ball sailed by.

"Strike one!" the umpire called.

The crowd booed.

Red held up his hand and then took two more practice swings.

A moment later, the pitcher threw again.

Red wasn't going to let it go this time. He dug down and swung as the ball shot over the plate. The bat chopped through the air and blasted into the ball.

But instead of flying toward the outfield wall, the ball launched almost straight up!

Red dropped his bat and ran for first base.

The Pirates catcher jumped out of his crouch, ran forward, held up his glove, and waited. The ball fell back down. Just as Red reached first base, the baseball dropped into the catcher's glove.

PLONK!

It was an out.

The inning was over. Red would have to wait until his next, and possibly final, at bat in the game to try to extend his hitting streak.

"Argh!" Mike said. "Red might only have one more chance to break the record!"

Kate pointed to the scoreboard. "But at least he still has a chance," she said. "And the Cardinals are only losing by one, so that's good."

"Well, you can't win on an empty stomach," Mike said. "Maybe it's a good time to get some food." He rubbed his belly. "I'm hungry!"

"It's not time to get food," Kate said. "We need to investigate the peanut butter!"

Mike sighed. He scuffed at the ground with his sneaker. "Okay," he said. "If we *have* to."

"Of course we have to," Kate said. "We have to find Louie before Red is at bat again!"

Mike straightened up. "Hey, I've got a *better* idea," he said. "What if we go find Harry the hot dog guy?"

"What's he going to know about the peanut butter?" Kate asked.

Mike shrugged. "I don't know," he said. "But *I* always work best on a full stomach! Let's get a hot dog and *then* investigate the peanut butter."

Kate smiled. "Actually, that's a *great* idea,"

she said, jumping up and down. "Maybe Harry knows something about the groundskeeper who was holding the jar of peanut butter!"

"Yahoo!" Mike said. "A new clue! And one that requires a stop at a hot dog stand to investigate! That's my favorite kind."

Kate rolled her eyes. "It always comes back to food for you, doesn't it?" she asked.

"It's dinnertime, and I'm hungry!" Mike said. "Hey, speaking of food. Do you know what they call a hot dog race?"

"No, what?" Kate asked.

"Wiener takes all!" Mike said.

Peanut Butter
Hot Dogs

Kate and Mike found Harry near the main entrance. The red-and-white-striped cart was filled with hot dogs, chips, and drinks. Harry was standing behind the cash register on the right side.

Mike and Kate stepped up to the cart.

"Hey, guys!" Harry said when he noticed them. "Hungry for some hot dogs? You've come to the right place. Oh, hang on!"

Harry grabbed a handful of napkins from the stand and turned around.

"Ah, ah, *achoooo*!" Harry sneezed. A few of the napkins fluttered away. Harry ran after them and scooped them up. He tossed them away and then rubbed some hand sanitizer on his hands.

"Sorry, it's my allergies. What can I get you?" he asked.

While Mike thought about whether he wanted a hot dog with ketchup, mustard, or both, he noticed a jar of crunchy peanut butter on the counter. "What's that for?" he asked.

Harry glanced down at the jar. He picked it up and moved it over to the side of the cart. "Oh, it's just peanut butter," he said. He shrugged. "Sometimes people want it on their hot dogs."

"Yuck!" Kate said. "That's gross!"

"Are you kidding? It's great," Harry said. "But maybe it's not for everyone." He looked at Mike. "What do you want on *your* hot dog?"

"Definitely *not* peanut butter!" Mike said. "I'll take one with mustard and relish. And a PowerPunch!"

"I'll have a hot dog with ketchup and onions," Kate said. "And a lemonade!"

"Coming right up!" Harry said. He prepped their two hot dogs and put them on the counter with the drinks. Kate handed him some money.

"So, Harry," Mike said. "Kate and I were thinking that one of the groundskeepers might have taken Louie. Before the game, there was one with a mustache who was eating peanut butter. Do you think he had anything to do with it?"

"Boots?" Harry asked. "Boots is the manager of the grounds crew. He's always dipping something into peanut butter. Celery, pretzels, broccoli. In fact, *he's* the one who likes peanut butter on his hot dogs! But I don't think he'd steal Louie."

"Did you happen to see any *other* grounds-keepers hanging around Louie?" Kate asked.

Harry leaned back for a moment and thought. Then he handed Kate her change and nodded. "You know, now that you mention it," he said, "I did see one in a red jacket petting Louie just before I left."

"Really?" Mike said. "We can check into that. It might be an important clue."

"No problem," Harry said. "Happy to help. I'd hate to see anything happen to that dog. How's Manny doing with the ransom?"

"Good, I think," Kate said. "He's working on it."

Harry nodded. "Great! I hope he's able to get a World Series trophy for Louie," he said. "At least the Cardinals have a bunch of them."

"I think he will," Mike said. He grabbed his hot dog and PowerPunch. "Well, thanks for helping."

Harry waved goodbye and turned to the next customer as Kate and Mike walked away, munching their food.

As they rounded the corner to head back to their seats, Kate started to make strange noises. "Humth! Humth!" Her mouth was full of hot dog. Mike stopped to see if she was choking.

Kate swallowed her bite of hot dog. "The ransom!" she cried.

Mike looked around. "What ransom?" he asked.

"Harry just asked about the ransom for Louie!" Kate said.

"So what?" Mike asked. "We told him about it when we saw him earlier."

Kate shook her head. "But we never said

what the ransom was!" she said. "We didn't say anything about the World Series trophy to Harry!"

Mike raised his eyebrows. "You mean—"

"Yes!" Kate said. "The only way Harry would know that the World Series trophy is the ransom is if *he's* the dog-napper!"

A Special Kind
of Hot Dog

"Wow!" Mike said. "Why would he do such a thing?"

"He's a huge Cardinals fan!" Kate said. "He told us that when he was looking at your Red Gibson signed ball. Remember how he said he'd like one? What if he *really* wants a Cardinals World Series trophy?"

"And he was there when Louie first escaped!" Mike said. "It definitely could be him! Good work!"

Mike gave Kate a high five.

"Thanks," Kate said. "But we still have to find Louie."

Mike and Kate peeked around the corner to watch Harry. He was helping a customer who had bought three hot dogs. There was one more customer in line.

"So, where do you think he put Louie?" Mike asked.

"That's what we need to find out, and fast," Kate said. "Maybe he put him in the storage room over there. Or in his car."

Kate glanced at the scoreboard. It was the bottom of the eighth inning, and St. Louis was batting. They were still behind by one run.

"We've got to find Louie before Red gets up again," Kate said. "Otherwise he'll still be too upset to break the record!"

Mike snapped his fingers. "We don't have time for the chief of security to investigate. We need to get Harry to tell us where Louie is right now," he said.

"How?" Kate asked.

"We'll just tell him that we know he's the dog-napper," Mike said. "But that we won't turn him in if he brings us to Louie. Then we can return Louie and tell Red that we've found him!"

Kate thought about it, and then nodded. "Great idea," she said. "It's more important to get Louie back than worry about turning Harry in to the police."

"Okay!" Mike said. He and Kate started walking to the hot dog stand. But as they turned the corner, Harry disappeared behind his hot dog cart.

"Ah, ah, *achoooooooo!*" Harry bent over in a sneezing fit. *"Achoooooooo! Achoooooooo!"*

He grabbed handfuls of napkins to sneeze into. The sneezes echoed down the hallway.

Kate grabbed Mike's arm and pulled him back around the corner.

"Hold on!" she said. "I've got a new plan. Harry's sneezing!"

"I know *that*," Mike said. "He's been sneezing all day."

"No! You're missing the point," Kate said. "He's sneezing. Remember when we were petting Louie and Harry looked at our signed

baseball? He sneezed! He said he was allergic to dogs!"

Harry sneezed again.

"That must be a bad allergy if he's been sneezing all this time," Mike said.

"No! That's not it!" Kate said. "He's sneezing *now* because Louie must be someplace nearby!"

Mike's eyes opened wide. "Wow! I'll bet you're right," he said. "But where?"

Mike and Kate peeked around the corner. Harry had stopped sneezing and was selling hot dogs to two little girls. When he was finished, Harry turned around and opened a door behind him. He went into what looked like a storage room and came out a moment later with packages of hot dog buns.

"Louie could be in that storage room!" Kate said.

"Or in that cooler," Mike said. He pointed

to a red cooler behind Harry. "It's big enough for Louie to fit in if he curled up. Maybe Harry drilled holes in the top so Louie would have air to breathe."

Mike tapped the wall with his finger. "How can we get Harry out of there so we can search for Louie?"

Kate thought for a moment.

"Well, we know he really wants that World Series trophy," Kate said. "What if we tell him that Manny needs his help with it? Then Harry will go down to the groundskeepers' area. That will give us at least ten minutes before he returns."

"But what happens when Manny *isn't* there asking for help with the trophy?" Mike asked. "Isn't he going to be mad at us?"

Kate shrugged. "It doesn't matter," she said. "Maybe he'll think we made a mistake. He'll probably just come back to his cart. All we need is a few minutes to find Louie."

They walked over to Harry's stand and waited for him to finish with a customer.

"Hungry for more already?" Harry asked when he spotted Kate and Mike.

Kate laughed. "No, but we just talked to Manny," she said. "He's down in the grounds-keepers' area and wanted to know if you could help him."

Harry glanced at the hot dog cart. He shook his head. "I don't know," he said. "I should really stay with the cart. Maybe he can get someone else."

"But Manny needs your help getting the World Series trophy ready for the dog-napper," Kate said.

Harry's eyes grew wide. "The trophy?"

he asked. "Really? I guess I could take a few minutes off." He nodded for a moment while he thought. Then he reached underneath the cart and pulled out a black-and-white sign. He set it on top of the counter and locked the cash register.

The sign read BACK IN 15 MINUTES.

"Thanks for letting me know," Harry said. "I'll be back shortly." He headed for the groundskeepers' area.

When Harry disappeared around the corner, Kate turned to Mike.

"*Quick!* We don't have much time!" she said. They turned and ran for the door to the supply room. Luckily, it wasn't locked. Mike pulled it open. Kate ducked inside and switched the light on.

The shelves inside were filled with supplies.

Big packages of rolls. Extra cardboard con-
tainers for the food. And lots of sauces. But
no dog!

Kate sighed. She turned the light off, and
they slipped outside.

Mike pointed to the red cooler. "Louie's got
to be in there!" he said. He leaned over and
pulled the top of the cooler up.

It was filled with plenty of drink bottles. But again, no dog!

"Aww!" Mike said. "Now what? Harry's going to be back soon, and we haven't found Louie!"

"Harry was sneezing. So Louie must be here. But where?" Kate said.

She and Mike studied the area. There wasn't anything around the hot dog cart except people passing by. There was a souvenir shop about a hundred feet away and a garbage can on the other side of the walkway.

As Mike looked around, he noticed the scoreboard. The Cardinals had just gotten the third out and were coming off the field to bat. "Uh-oh," Mike said. "Red's going to be up soon! And the game's tied! If Red doesn't get a hit, his streak will be over!"

Kate tapped the ground with her foot.

"Think. Think. Think," she said under her breath. "Where did Harry hide him?"

The glittery silver Gateway Arch caught Mike's eye. "Well, if we were over at the Arch, I know where I would have hidden Louie," he said. "In one of those little tram cars! I sure felt trapped in them this morning."

Kate stopped tapping. "What did you say?" she asked.

Mike looked at her. "You heard me," he said. He pointed to the Arch. "If we were over there, I would have hidden Louie in a tram car! They're like little metal boxes."

Kate's eyebrows went up. "Brilliant, Mike!" she said. "I think that's it!"

"What's it?" Mike asked. "You think Louie is trapped on the Arch? That's a bit far for Harry to go during the game."

Kate rolled her eyes. "No! Look at this,"

she said. She pointed to Harry's cart. "What's that?" she asked.

Mike looked at her funny. "A hot dog cart?" he asked slowly.

Kate shook her head. She pointed to a door on the right side of the back of the cart. "No, what's that?" she asked.

Mike studied the door. It was about two feet by two feet. "A door to a small metal box on the hot dog cart?"

"Bingo!" Kate said. "It's a supply cabinet, but I'm pretty sure it doesn't have supplies in it today! Let's see what's inside."

Mike leaned over and turned the latch on the door.

It didn't move.

"It's locked!" Mike said.

Kate tried the handle, but it didn't budge.

"We don't have a lot of time," Mike said.

He searched the ground behind them. "Quick! Find a rock or something hard and I'll smash it open."

"No, I've got a better idea," Kate said. She reached over to the other side of the cart and picked up a small skewer with grilled peppers and onions on it. Kate slid the food off the skewer and wiped it on a nearby rag. Then she slipped the end of the skewer into the lock.

"What are you doing?" Mike asked.

Kate jiggled the sliver of metal inside the lock. "Picking the lock," she said. "It looks pretty basic." She moved the skewer back and forth inside the lock while lightly pressing on the door handle.

"Hey, where'd you learn how to do that?" Mike asked.

Kate glanced over her shoulder at him. "Where do you think?" she said. "From a book, of course! I've been reading about Harry Houdini. He was famous for picking locks, and it sounded like fun to me. So I've been practicing at home."

Kate poked one more time, and the latch turned! The cabinet door swung wide open.

Two eyes peeked up at Kate and Mike.

Then a furry nose poked out, and a big wet tongue gave them both big wet kisses!

A Dog Whistle

It was Louie!

He was curled up on his bed inside the hot dog cart's storage area. There was even a red chew toy in front of him, filled with peanut butter. While Mike and Kate stared at him, Louie tried to lick the peanut butter out of the chew toy.

"Well, he's not in a rush to get out," Mike said. "I guess he's comfortable."

Kate nodded. She pointed to the far side of the compartment. "That's good. At least there's a bowl of water in there for him," she said.

"And peanut butter in the chew toy!" Mike said. "I'll bet Harry used the peanut butter to lure Louie into the cart when no one was looking. He probably dropped some on the floor. The groundskeeper we saw with the jar of peanut butter didn't have anything to do with it!"

"I think you're right," Kate said. She glanced around. There was no sign of Harry. "We need to get Louie out of here and tell Red that we found him!"

Kate leaned over again and gently pulled on Louie's collar. He gave his peanut butter chew toy one more lick and then hopped out of the hot dog cart. Kate closed the door and held on tight to Louie's collar while Mike went to look for something to use as a leash.

A few moments later, Mike was back. "I couldn't find a leash," he said. "So I made one!"

He held up a leash made from two shoelaces tied together. He was holding his sneakers in the other hand, since they wouldn't stay on his feet without the laces.

"Great idea!" Kate said.

They tied the shoelaces to Louie's collar.

"Okay, come on, boy!" Kate said. "We've got to get a message to Red right away!"

"And we've got to get away from this hot dog cart before Harry returns!" Mike said.

Mike, Kate, and Louie jogged through the stadium toward the seats near the Cardinals' dugout. The first Cardinals batter of the inning was at the plate. Red would be up next!

They had to slow down to a walk as they got closer. On the field, the St. Louis batter hit a double! The game was still tied. The crowd went wild with cheers. The fans started clapping and chanting Red's name. A good hit by Red would send that runner home and put the Cardinals ahead to win the game!

"Come on!" Kate said to Mike. She pointed to an aisle leading to the field. "We'll bring Louie to the fence near the on-deck circle so Red can see him!"

Red took a few practice swings while the runner dusted himself off.

Mike and Kate started down the aisle.

"*Stop!* Hold it right there!" said a voice.

Mike, Kate, and Louie stopped and turned. A security guard stood at the top of the aisle. In their hurry, they hadn't seen him.

"You can't go to those seats unless you have tickets," the security guard said. "And you definitely can't bring a dog!"

Kate pointed to the batting circle. "But we're friends with Red!" she said. "We have to show him something before he bats! Otherwise he might not keep his hitting streak alive!"

The guard looked at Red and then back at Mike and Kate. He shook his head.

"No! I don't care who you are friends with," he said. "Stadium rules do not allow a dog in the stands."

Kate stepped closer to the guard. "But we *have* to get a message to Red!"

The guard shrugged. "Not with that dog, you're not," he said. "And not without tickets. Sorry! Move along. You can't block the aisle."

Mike looked at the field. Red was headed for home plate!

"Red's going to bat! And he doesn't know we found Louie!" Mike cried. "We've got to do something!"

Red stopped just outside the batter's box. It looked like he was thinking.

Mike tried to push past the security guard. But the guard stood his ground.

"Back! Now!" the guard ordered. "Or I'll have you removed from the stadium!"

Red wiped his cleats in the dirt outside the batter's box. He was just about to step inside when Kate put two fingers in her mouth and blew with all her might.

A shrill whistle pierced the air.

Red looked up from the field.

"I knew that learning to whistle really loudly would pay off!" Kate said. She nudged Mike. "Quick! Yell with me!"

Mike and Kate moved to the side of the security guard and yelled together at the top of their lungs, *"RED! RED! RED!"*

Kate gave another long, loud whistle.

Red looked directly at them. Mike bent down and picked Louie up, then lifted him as high as he could!

A huge smile spread across Red's face! He clapped his hands together, then thumped his heart with one hand and pointed at Louie. His smile couldn't have been bigger.

Red stepped into the batter's box to hit.

A Doggone
Good Idea

The security guard stared at Mike with Louie snuggled in his arms. Then he looked down at Red at the plate. "Hmph!" he grunted.

Red took a few more practice swings. He glanced back at Mike, Kate, and Louie and smiled again. Then he adjusted his gloves and took another swing.

Mike set Louie down on the ground. He held his shoelace leash tight.

"Okay, you two can stand over there to watch Red bat," the guard said. "But you can't go down the aisle."

"Thank you," Kate said.

They moved a few steps to the left, behind the last row of seats. They had a perfect view of the field. Louie curled up at Mike's feet.

Kate took out her phone. She started to dial.

"What are you doing?" Mike asked. "Red's batting!"

Kate glanced at Mike. "I know!" she said. "But we've got to call Manny to tell him we have Louie and that he shouldn't turn over the trophy!"

Mike blushed. "Oh," he said. "Okay, good idea!"

Kate connected with Manny. A few moments later, she hung up. "It's all set," she said. "He's calling security to find Harry. He's not going to turn over the trophy. He was so happy that we found Louie!"

Red rested his bat on the ground and adjusted his batting gloves again. Then he picked up his bat and stared down the pitcher.

The Pirates pitcher hurled the ball at the plate.

Red let the pitch go by.

"Strike one!" the umpire called.

The crowd groaned. Then they cheered louder for Red. Mike and Kate clapped and jumped up and down.

The pitcher threw again.

It looked like Red was going to let this one go by, too. He hesitated a moment, but then he swung. *WHACK!*

The force of the blow swung the bat around in front of Red. He held on to it with his left hand as the bat circled behind him. He stood at home plate and watched the ball.

The ball sailed over the pitcher's head.

It climbed high into the night sky.

It looked like it was headed straight for the windows at the top of the Gateway Arch!

Red dropped the bat and ran for first base. The runner on second headed for third.

The fans went crazy.

"Go! Go! Go!" Mike yelled.

"Run!" Kate called.

Red and the other runner circled the bases. The ball leveled off and flew toward the Arch.

Mike and Kate waved their arms and screamed, *"Go!"*

The first runner crossed home plate!

Red rounded second! He kept going!

The ball dropped down. It landed in the outfield seats and bounced once before a fan snagged it.

Home run!

Red crossed home plate.

The Cardinals had won!

Red had set the record!

And Louie was safe!

After the game, Red wanted to see Louie. That's how Mike, Kate, Louie, Red, and Manny ended up back in the groundskeepers' area. Manny was getting ready to go, but he couldn't leave until Red stopped petting Louie.

"Where did you find him?" Red asked in between nuzzles with Louie.

"In Harry's hot dog cart!" Mike said.

"I can't believe it," Red said. "A *hot* dog in a hot dog cart! I'm so happy you found him!"

"And *we're* happy we found him in time for you to set the hitting record!" Kate said.

Red smiled. "It was nice to set the record!" he said. "But I'm happier that you rescued Louie. Maybe if he comes to my next game, I'll set another record!" Red leaned over and gave Louie a hug.

"What happened to Harry?" Red asked.

"He's sold his last hot dog here," Manny said. He glanced at Mike and Kate. "Apparently, *someone* told him I was looking for help with the ransom. Harry went downstairs to look for me. But when he didn't find me, he went back up to his cart. I have no idea when he noticed that Louie wasn't there."

"How did you catch him?" Mike asked.

"Well, I was just about to put the latest Cardinals' World Series trophy in the drop-off place when Kate called and told me that Harry was the dog-napper," Manny said. "Mr. Lee and his security team stopped Harry as soon as he got near the statue. I guess that even without Louie, Harry was trying to pick up the trophy. The police will be here soon to arrest him."

"At least he took good care of Louie," Kate said. "He was very cozy inside that hot dog cart."

"Yes, that's good," Manny said. "But he shouldn't have taken him at all."

Louie stood up and gave Red's face a big lick with his tongue. Then he shook all over and walked to Kate and Mike. He circled them once and then lay in front of them.

Mike and Kate dropped to their knees to pet him.

"Louie really likes you two," Manny said. "How about the next time you're in town, we let you ride up front with Louie when we parade around the stadium. How would you like that?"

"That would be great!" Kate said.

Everyone looked at Mike. He seemed lost in thought. Kate nudged him. "Are you still with us? How does that sound to you?"

Mike remained still for a moment, and then a big smile spread across his face. "We'd *paws*-itively love to do it!" he said with a nod. "That's a doggone good idea!"

Manny, Red, and Kate laughed. And Louie rolled over on his back so Mike could scratch his belly!

BALL·PARK Mysteries

Dugout Notes

☆ St. Louis Cardinals ☆

Famous Birds: Stan, Bob, Dizzy, and Daffy. Cardinals fans have had many great players to root for over the years. Stan Musial was one of the best hitters of all time. His nickname was Stan the Man. Bob Gibson was a great pitcher. The Cardinals player with the wackiest name was Dizzy Dean. His real name was Jay, but Dizzy was his nickname. He pitched thirty winning games in 1934. His brother Paul was also on the team. Paul's nickname was Daffy!

A Cardinal lowers the mound. Bob Gibson was such a good pitcher that major-league baseball had to change the field to keep the game interesting! After Gibson posted an ERA (earned run average) of 1.12 in 1968, baseball officials decided to lower the height of the pitching mound from fifteen inches to ten inches. That gave pitchers less of an advantage and made it a bit easier for batters to hit the ball.

So many World Series trophies! As of the 112th World Series, the St. Louis Cardinals have won the second most trophies (behind the New York Yankees). They won their first in 1926 against the Yankees.

Cardinals before they were Cardinals.
The St. Louis Cardinals started off as the St. Louis Brown Stockings in 1875. In 1883, they shortened their name to the Browns. (Later, there was another St. Louis baseball team named the Browns. It became the Baltimore Orioles.) The team became the Perfectos for one year and started wearing uniforms with bright red, or cardinal, trim. A newspaper writer, Willie McHale, reported that he heard a woman say that the new uniforms were "a lovely shade of cardinal." He used it in his writing, and fans liked it. The next year, the team officially became the St. Louis Cardinals.

Lots of bird names. The St. Louis Cardinals have had a lot of nicknames over the years: the Cards, the Redbirds, the Birds, the Birds on a Bat, the Birdinals, the Card Birds, the Running Redbirds, the Gashouse Gang, and more.

Their very own Hall of Fame. The National Baseball Hall of Fame is in Cooperstown, New York (where Mike and Kate live). But the Cardinals have their own Hall of Fame directly across the street from their stadium. It houses an incredible collection of items from St. Louis baseball history. You can see (and possibly even hold!) bats used by famous Cardinals such as Stan Musial.

Clydesdales, dogs, and delivery wagons.
For many years, the Cardinals were owned
by the Anheuser-Busch brewing company,
which is in St. Louis. In 1933, Anheuser-
Busch started using a team of Clydesdale
horses pulling a delivery wagon in its adver-
tisements. Today, the company has multi-
ple teams, or hitches, of horses that travel
the country with Dalmatian dogs riding in
the wagon. The horses weigh up to 2,300
pounds each. A single horse can eat as much
as sixty pounds of hay per day and drink
thirty gallons of water!

The Gashouse Gang. The 1934 Cardinals
were known as the Gashouse Gang. They
won ninety-five games that year (that's
really good!) and beat the Detroit Tigers in
the World Series. They played aggressive

baseball and weren't afraid to get their uniforms dirty. The nickname Gashouse refers to people from rough-and-tumble city neighborhoods near power plants.

Enos's mad dash. In 1946, the Cardinals beat the Boston Red Sox to win the World Series with a spectacular play. Enos Slaughter scored the winning run by dashing from first base to home on a double by Harry Walker. Boston's shortstop, Johnny Pesky, hesitated on his throw to home, and Enos crossed the plate to win the game.

A one-stadium World Series. St. Louis was home to a one-stadium World Series. In 1944, the St. Louis

Cardinals played the St. Louis Browns (the team that's now the Baltimore Orioles) for the World Series. They shared Sportsman's Park as their stadium, so that's where all the World Series games happened that year. The Cardinals won, four games to two.

Bird rivals. Some of the Cardinals' biggest rivals over the years have been the Chicago Cubs, the Cincinnati Reds, and the Los Angeles Dodgers.